DINOSAUR WORLD

By Geoffrey T. Williams
Illustrated by Borje Svensson

PRICE STERN SLOAN, INC.

MW00916285

Lost In Dinosaur World can be read with
its accompanying word-for-word audiocassette
to create an exciting, educational adventure
into the past.

FOURTH PRINTING — SEPTEMBER 1987

Copyright © 1987 by Geoffrey T. Williams
Illustrations copyright © 1987 by Price Stern Sloan, Inc.
Published by Price Stern Sloan, Inc.
360 North La Cienega Boulevard, Los Angeles, California 90048

ISBN: 0-8431-1878-4

Timothy McDunn was dressed for *adventure*. He was wearing hiking boots, rugged-looking pants, a camouflage-colored shirt and an old floppy hat borrowed from Grandpa McDunn. He had binoculars hanging around his neck and he was just buckling a survival kit to his belt when his mother came in. She smiled. "We're just going to Dinosaur World, Tim. Not to the jungle or someplace dangerous."

"You never can tell," was all he said.

Out in the hallway, Mr. McDunn was looking for something. "We can't leave for Dinosaur World until I find my coat."

Mary McDunn, Tim's sister, opened the closet door. "Here it is, Dad. Can we go now?"

"As soon as I find my keys." Mary reached into the coat pocket and handed her father the keys to the car. "Uh...thanks. Now, just one more thing...where's your little brother?"

Mary opened the closet door again. "Well, he's not in here."

Mr. McDunn smiled. "Very funny." Just then Tim and Mrs. McDunn came into the room. "There you are. Ready for your first visit to Dinosaur World, Tim?"

"You bet!"

Outside, Dad started the car. "What's the first thing you want to do?"

Tim didn't hesitate for a second. "Ride the T-Rex Express!"

"Of course," said his father.

"And then I want to see an allosaur!"

Mr. McDunn laughed. "Somehow I knew you'd want to see the scariest animal in the park."

Dinosaur World looked and sounded exactly the way Tim thought it should: tall pines rising overhead, along with exotic ferns, ginkgo and monkey puzzle trees; giant pterosaurs and pteranodons circling in the blue sky, their eerie, high-pitched squeals carrying across the distance; roars, grunts and growls coming from deep in the forest, made by who-knows-what-kind of wild creatures; rumblings and puffs of grey smoke and steam curling from the top of a small volcano.

The girl at the entrance gave them each a ticket and a beautiful color map of the park. Then she handed Mr. McDunn a small box with an antenna. "Here's your radio guide. Any questions you have about the animals, he'll be able to answer. If you're walking, stay on the marked paths. If you're riding the T-Rex Express, keep your arms and legs inside — and please, don't feed the dinosaurs."

Tim laughed, "Who could ever get close enough to a dinosaur to feed it?"

Dad asked, "Where to first?"

And Tim shouted, "The T-Rex Express!"

And Mary said, "The Petting Zoo!"

But a small, thin-sounding voice said, "I'd suggest the protoceratops hatchlings."

Tim looked surprised. "Who said that?"

"The radio guide," Mary told her brother. "Listen."

"If you're interested in the family life of dinosaurs, the Nursery is right next to the Petting Zoo, on the way to the T-Rex Express. Ten of the eggs hatched last week. Szechuan, the mother protoceratops, is very proud of her babies."

Tim was getting impatient. "I don't want to see a bunch of eggs."

"Tim, it won't take but a few minutes, and I'm sure there'll be plenty of exciting things for you to do today." Little did Mr. McDunn know how true that was.

Suddenly, Tim stopped and pointed. "Wow! Look at that!" The biggest animal he had ever seen had wandered over to some nearby trees and was noisily eating the leaves.

"That's our brachiosaur," their guide explained. "His name means 'arm lizard'. See how his front legs are taller than his

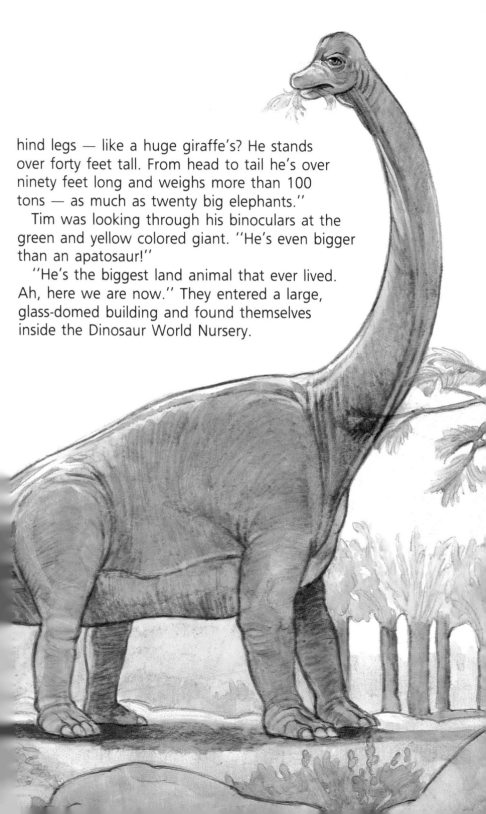

hind legs — like a huge giraffe's? He stands over forty feet tall. From head to tail he's over ninety feet long and weighs more than 100 tons — as much as twenty big elephants."

Tim was looking through his binoculars at the green and yellow colored giant. "He's even bigger than an apatosaur!"

"He's the biggest land animal that ever lived. Ah, here we are now." They entered a large, glass-domed building and found themselves inside the Dinosaur World Nursery.

The air was warm and humid, and the sunlight coming through the glass roof lit the area with a soft, yellow glow.

It made an interesting scene — the McDunn family standing at the Nursery window watching the dinosaur family.

The radio guide's voice echoed strangely in the room. "Protoceratops are the earliest known horned dinosaurs. They're like triceratops, but not nearly as big."

Tim wasn't very impressed. "They sure don't have very big horns." He watched the six-foot-long, 3,000-pound mother, Szechuan, nuzzle a few of the football-sized eggs that lay in

the nest while ten tiny babies squirmed and squealed in the sand nearby.

Mary thought they were cute. "Oh, look. They're so tiny."

Mrs. McDunn looked at her daughter. "No! Absolutely not! You are not going to bring one of those home!"

"Uh...I think it's about time to get on board the T-Rex Express," said Mr. McDunn.

The T-Rex Express was one of the most popular attractions in the park. It was a train shaped just like a fierce tyrannosaurus rex. People could buy tickets and ride through all the different areas where the dinosaurs lived, watching the huge animals from the safety and comfort of the train.

Tim bought a ticket for the "SuperTour" — a journey through the Triassic, Jurassic and Cretaceous eras — all the periods of time during which dinosaurs lived. He meant to see *everything* in one day. His mom and dad and sister just bought tickets through the Triassic. After that Tim would be on his own. He was very excited.

Finally the whistle blew, steam curled from the nose of the T-Rex engine and he was off on his trip through Dinosaur World, comfortably inside one of the most ferocious carnivores ever to roam the earth.

The train wound through the ancient Triassic landscape —
on one side was the swamp that bordered Dinosaur Sea.
Strange, stunted trees and ferns poked up through the sand
and mud; a crocodile, floating lazily in the water, hissed as
they passed; a small pterosaur glided by, his long, leathery
wings slowly flapping as he flew out over the sea to fish
with his narrow, pelican-like beak.

The train crossed a bridge and slowed near some rocks by
the shore.

Suddenly, several of the passengers screamed and Mr.
McDunn yelled, "Look out!"

Tim looked quickly around and saw a giant spray of water
erupt as a huge creature lunged onto the rocks right next to
the train.

The dinosaur landed on his big front flippers and gave a
piercing cry. Tim was startled, but tried not to show it.
"What is that?"

"A nothosaur," the radio guide answered. "An amphibious
reptile, about twenty-five feet long. He lives part of the time
in the water and part of the time on land. But he doesn't
usually come this close to the train. Careful, don't lean too
far out of the window."

The sea serpent's long, curved neck swayed like a snake. The thin head came closer and closer, until Tim could hear him breathe and see water dripping from his needle-sharp teeth. Then, without warning, the nothosaur gave another ear-splitting shriek and slipped back under the water, leaving the boy a little frightened and wondering how much excitement the rest of the trip would bring.

On the other side of the train stretched a dry, rocky plain that looked like a prehistoric desert. As they slowed down, a lizard, about ten feet long, slithered out from behind some big rocks. He had a tall sail, like a big fin, running all along his back. "What kind of dinosaur is that?"

"A dimetrodon. Technically, because he has a different kind of bone structure, he's not really a dinosaur at all—just a big lizard."

"Is his sail only for decoration?"

"No. Dimetrodons are *ectothermic* — that means cold-blooded. They need heat from the sun to live, but too much sun makes them overheat, so scientists think reptiles like the dimetrodon used their sails to help regulate body temperature."

"Aren't dinosaurs ecto...ecto... What was that?"

"Ectothermic."

"Thanks. Aren't they all cold-blooded, too?"

"Scientists used to think so. But after a lot of studying, they now think dinosaurs were warm-blooded, or *endothermic.*"

"Gee. Just like people," Tim said.

The train stopped at the end of the Triassic tour and Mr. and Mrs. McDunn and Mary got out.

Mr. McDunn looked serious as he handed Tim the radio. "This is your first trip here, so be very careful not to lose your guide. Whatever you need to know, just ask. And remember, no matter what happens, don't get off the train." Then they all waved goodbye. Tim watched until they disappeared from sight around a curve. He couldn't help feeling just a little lonesome as he continued his adventure.

As the trip through the Jurassic started, he noticed the scenery changing: plants grew thicker — more like a jungle, there were more palm trees, bigger ferns, even some pine trees.

Several long-necked diplodocus were wading at the shallow edge of the swamp, their huge tails stirring the muddy water from side to side.

"Diplodocus had very lightweight bones, so even though they were eighty or ninety feet long, they only weighed as much as a couple of elephants."

This map to Dinosaur World
belongs to: _____

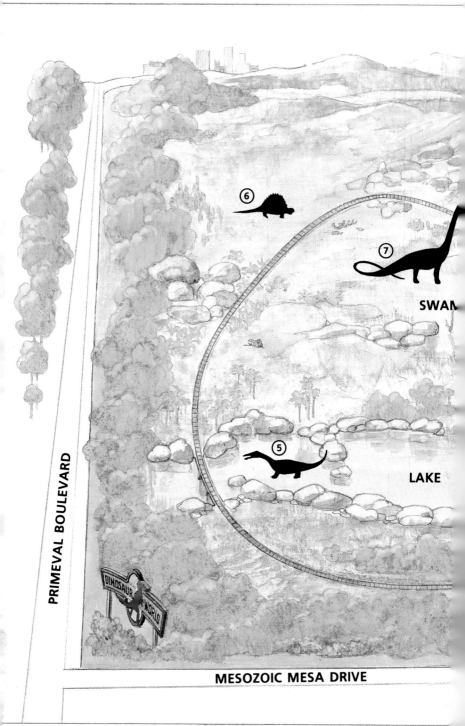

1. BRACHIOSAUR (BRAK·ee·uh·SOR)
2. PTERANODON (tuh·RAN·uh·DON)
3. PTEROSAUR (TER·uh·SOR)
4. PROTOCERATOPS (pro·toe·SER·uh·tops)
5. NOTHOSAUR (NOTH·oh·SOR)
6. DIMETRODON (die·MET·ruh·don)
7. DIPLODOCUS (di·PLOD·uh·kus)
8. STEGOSAUR (STEG·uh·SOR)
9. BABY PARASAUROLOPHUS (par·uh·sor·AH·luf·us)
10. ARCHAEOPTERYX (AR·kee·OP·ter·iks)
11. ALLOSAUR (AL·oh·SOR)
12. ICHTHYOSAUR (IK·thee·uh·SOR)
13. PARASAUROLOPHUS (par·uh·sor·AH·luf·us)

We hope you enjoy your adventure in Dinosaur World. For your own safety, please remember these important rules:

   1. Do not leave the T-Rex Express while the tour is in progress.
   2. When walking, stay on the marked paths.
   3. *Do not feed the dinosaurs!*

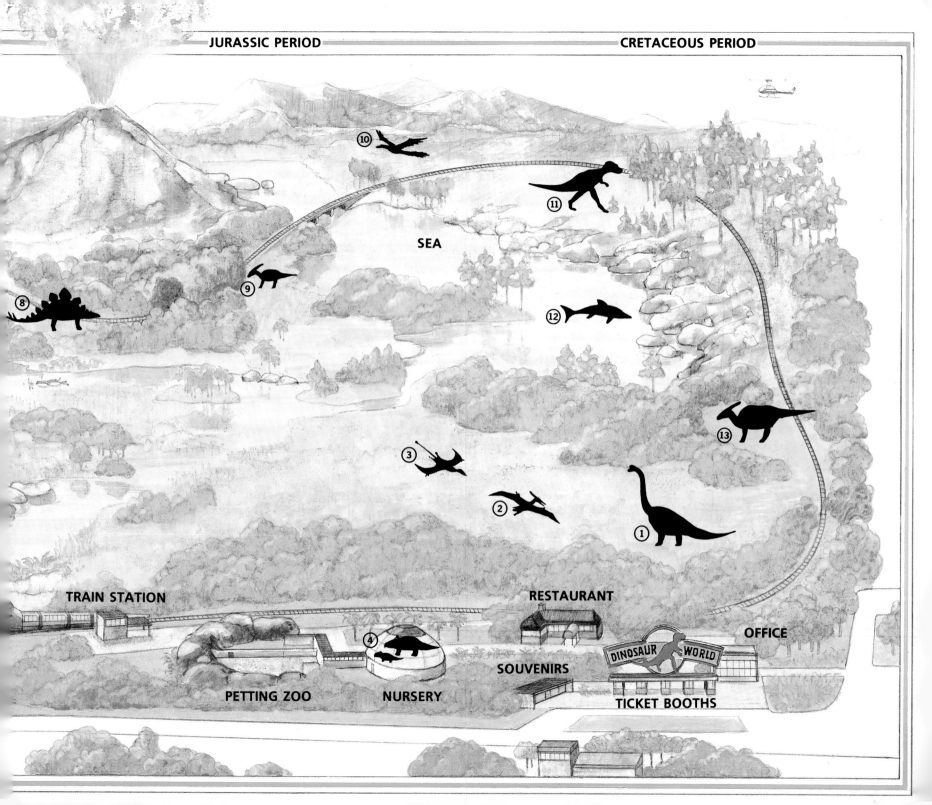

Just then, as he listened to the guide, Tim did something that would change his whole day. He set the radio down on the windowsill, leaned out, and lifted the binoculars to his eyes.

"I can't see the diplodocus very well."

"Careful!" But the guide's warning came too late.

"Oh, no!" Tim accidentally bumped the radio. It clattered down the embankment by the side of the tracks and came to rest almost under the tail of a huge stegosaur, where it made sputtering and buzzing noises.

Almost without thinking, Tim jumped out and scrambled down the embankment. Passengers in the other cars were busy watching the diplodocus, so no one saw him leave the train. In a few steps he reached the radio.

The thirty-foot stegosaur was eating. Tim was close enough to touch her. So he did. Wouldn't you? He reached out, and very softly touched one of her tree-trunk-sized legs.

The skin felt thick and wrinkled, like an elephant's, but without any hair. A ripple went up the stegosaur's back, along the large bony plates used for defense against attacking carnivores. Her tail shook, and the dangerous spikes on the end rattled ominously. She turned her head to look at the odd little human creature. Tim quickly pulled his hand back. He must not have looked very threatening because, after a moment, the stegosaur went right on eating.

Tim picked up the radio. It was dirty and the antenna was bent. He shook it and heard an electronic buzzing. Was it broken? Then he heard

something else. Something that immediately made him forget the radio and the huge dinosaur.

As he looked up, he saw the T-Rex Express disappear from sight down the tracks. The train was leaving without him!

He scrambled back up the embankment and began running along behind it, yelling, "Wait! Hey! Wait for me!"

He stood panting, completely out of breath, helplessly watching as the train disappeared around a bend. A puff of smoke was the last thing he saw of the T-Rex Express. From far away, a lonely whistle echoed back down the empty tracks.

Without any warning, almost by accident it seemed, he was alone — lost in the middle of Dinosaur World.

In those first few moments, Tim came very close to being afraid. The stegosaur had stopped chewing and was looking at him; the huge diplodocus had twisted their long necks around and were gazing in his direction. From the depths of the jungle some ferocious creature roared and Tim could hear it crashing through the undergrowth. He hoped it wasn't coming his way. The sounds grew more distant and soon the dinosaurs went back to eating. Tim sighed with relief and began thinking about what to do next.

"*Bzzt hazzbt?*" said a little voice. Tim held the radio up. "*Wrrzz weet?*" Sure enough, sounds were coming from it. He jiggled it. "What happened? Where are we?"

"I accidentally dropped you off the train. I got off to get you and the train left without me."

The guide moaned. "Oh, no. Uh...how fast can you run?"

"Why?"

"Because you don't want to get caught out here when *the allosaur zzz bzzt ssstrt grrx.*" The words faded away in a crackle of static.

Tim shook it. "What? Caught out here when the allosaur what?" But nothing more came out.

He began walking along the tracks, keeping a sharp eye out for anything that stood over twenty feet tall, had teeth like steak knives and a disposition like a bucket of rattlesnakes. In other words, anything that looked like an allosaur.

From the safety of the train it had all been so different. But now Dinosaur World seemed mysterious. Strange. Perhaps even...dangerous.

He came to a place where the trees arched over the tracks, making a dim, green tunnel.

He made his way quietly and cautiously, but when the bushes next to him started shaking violently, he yelled, "Yikes!" And when he heard a high, loud squeal, he ran and hid behind a giant tree fern.

The bushes shook some more, and then out walked the strangest dinosaur Tim had ever seen.

He was little. Not any taller than Tim. His stout, round body was colored in green and orange patches and he waddled on strong hind legs, using his tail for balance.

But the strangest thing about the little dinosaur was his head. He had a flat yellow beak like a duck, big, round eyes, and a weird tube, or horn, which curved back over his head about two feet.

The radio came to life with a crackle. *"Zzbsts.* It's a baby parasaurolophus."

"A para-what?" Tim asked in a whisper.

"A duckbill dinosaur. Parasaurolophus."

"Why's he making that noise?"

"He's probably lost and is calling for his mother. See if he'll eat some leaves. It might make him feel better."

"Don't feed the dinosaurs," the ticket girl had said. He never expected to get close enough to be able to. But then, he never expected to get lost either. He picked some tender leaves and held them out. The dinosaur took a nervous step backwards, looking at Tim with big, moist eyes. Then very slowly, he came closer and began nibbling. He was hungry. His eyes never left the boy.

When he was done he gave a soft *bleet* and backed away. Tim was amazed. "Wow. I've never fed a dinosaur before."

The radio guide warned him, "If we ever find his mother, don't try to feed her."

"Why not?"

"Because she's taller than your house."

When Tim walked out from under the trees he looked back and saw the baby dinosaur following. He tried to shoo him away. "Go on. Go look for your mother. Don't follow me, I'm lost, too." But the dinosaur stayed right behind, sometimes waddling along on his hind legs, sometimes hopping on all fours. After awhile Tim decided it was nice to have the company. He didn't feel quite so alone.

They were walking beside some tall pine trees when something made a ferocious cawing sound.

"Get down!" shouted the radio guide.

Tim barely had time to move as a brightly colored bird flew over his head and landed a few yards away. When he looked closer, he wasn't sure it was a bird at all. The creature had a head like a snake, and pointed teeth. But he had feet like a bird, and long, sharp claws that grew out of his wings.

"What kind of bird is that?"

"An archaeopteryx. I guess you'd call him a dinosaur-bird. The first bird-like animal that ever lived. They can't really fly. They climb trees and glide down, like flying squirrels." Just then, another one of the crow-sized creatures sailed down, landing next to the first, and together they raced off, their brilliant feathers spread out, noisily chasing some small lizards for dinner.

The baby dinosaur began to make a high, whining sound and looked around nervously. Tim asked the radio guide about it.

''His nose is very sensitive. Maybe he smells something dangerous and is frightened.''

''Well, *I* don't smell anything....'' But at that moment the duckbill gave a terrified scream and set off running.

Tim heard an awesome roar from very nearby, and suddenly everything seemed to happen at once.

''Run!'' squawked the guide. ''Run!''

Crash! Crunch! The ground shook as a giant allosaur thundered through the trees! It immediately caught sight of the small boy and the little dinosaur. With a mighty leap and an ear-splitting howl, it came straight for them.

Tim's heart was racing like mad. He'd never been so frightened in his life. ''Where do I run?''

"Follow the baby dinosaur!" Instinctively, the baby knew the only chance was to get to Dinosaur Sea ahead of the allosaur.

Tim ran like the wind. Faster than he had ever run before. He looked over his shoulder and saw trees and brush crumble as the monstrous beast pounded after them. Could he possibly make it to safety? How could an animal so big run so fast? How much further did he have to go? He could feel the allosaur's breath hot on his neck.

"Jump!" shouted the guide and Tim launched himself over the rocks and fell into Dinosaur Sea with a loud splash.

When he came up for air he was looking into the face of the enraged allosaur. The carnivorous beast was furious at seeing his dinner just out of reach. His hisses and roars filled the air as he stomped back and forth.

With a last futile try, the dinosaur leaned over the rocks and snapped his gaping jaws together. By accident, one of his long teeth hit the edge of a rock. With a loud *snap* the tooth broke off, falling right into Tim's upraised hand.

With the sputtering radio clutched in one hand and the eight-inch-long dinosaur tooth in the other, Tim was having a difficult time swimming.

The parasaurolophus, meanwhile, was doing much better. So Tim reached out and put an arm around his long neck. The baby didn't seem to mind helping the boy at all. He just *quacked* and towed Tim along.

They were swimming parallel to the shoreline, looking for a safe place to land, when a dark grey and blue shape exploded out of the water right next to them. The baby dinosaur kept right on swimming, paying no attention to the commotion.

"What the heck was that?" Tim wasn't ready for another surprise so soon.

The radio crackled to life. "An ichthyosaur. Very much like a modern dolphin, only bigger." This particular one was about thirty feet long.

He surfaced next to Tim and seemed friendly and curious. He gave a whistling cry, and splashed the boy and the small dinosaur playfully before diving deep into the water.

Just when Tim began to think the ichthyosaur had left them, the ocean erupted like a giant fountain and the powerful creature leaped high out of the sea once again, sending water spraying all around, shimmering like a rainbow in the sunlight. Tim laughed out loud.

Finally, the boy and the dinosaur emerged on a sandy beach far away from the roaring allosaur. Tim put the tooth in his pants pocket.

"Now that we're in the Cretaceous era," the radio said, "there's a chance tyrannosaurus rex himself could show up. We better get out of here."

Just then the baby gave another loud squeal. "Oh, no. Not again." Tim was getting ready to dive back in the ocean when he looked up and saw a much larger parasaurolophus coming out of the trees.

"Must be his mother," said the radio guide. "Better stay out of her way." The huge duck-billed dinosaur, big as a bus, with a horn more than six feet long curving over her head, bent down and began nuzzling her baby and honking. Then together they turned and waddled into the forest and were lost to sight.

Tim waved and felt like he was saying goodbye to a friend. Now he was alone again. He dug through his soggy survival kit, finally coming up with an old chocolate bar. He peeled the damp wrapper and began chewing. Soon, feeling

a little better, he set off once more down the tracks of the T-Rex Express. "Why hasn't anyone found me yet?" he asked the radio guide.

"I don't know. They should be here anytime now."

Ahead, the Cretaceous forest became even thicker. Swamp cypress and fir trees grew up to the water's edge, and Tim noticed colorful flowers here and there. Herons perched on spindly legs in the shallow water, ducks swam nearby and a flock of gulls flew overhead.

All of a sudden, from out of the trees ahead came another huge creature.

Not another hungry meat-eater! Tim was just too tired to run and hide. But wait a minute. What kind of dinosaur was this? When it roared, steam actually came out of its nostrils!

Tim stopped and stared as the monster came at him.

The radio snapped and popped some more and said, "It's a zzzt bst."

"What did you say?" asked Tim.

The radio crackled again. "I said 'it's about time'."

Tim looked more carefully, and saw that the "monster" bearing down on them was really just the front of the T-Rex Express. Someone had finally come to get him!

He sighed tiredly. "My folks will be so relieved to see me again."

A few minutes later he was back on Mesozoic Mesa.

The first thing he saw was his father, munching happily on a hot dog. Then he saw Mary standing at the Nursery window, and his mother looking over the fence at the babies in the Petting Zoo.

Tim was amazed. They didn't even know he'd been gone. They didn't know a thing about his adventure! He couldn't believe it!

Mr. McDunn put an arm around his son's shoulder. "So, was your SuperTour everything you wanted? Did you get to see any animals up close? Tell me all about it."

As they walked back to the parking lot, the roars and growls of the wild animals filled the air behind them. The T-Rex Express whistle sounded. Another trainload of passengers was setting off — each visitor about to experience his or her own special adventure in Dinosaur World.

Would Tim's family ever believe his adventure?

Then he felt the sharp point of the allosaur tooth safe in his pocket, and he smiled....